SCARY GRAPHICS

THE HAUNTED HIGH-TOPS

STONE ARCH BOOKS
a capstone imprint

Scary Graphics is published by Stone Arch Books,
an imprint of Capstone.
1710 Roe Crest Drive
North Mankato, Minnesota 56003
www.capstonepub.com

Library of Congress Cataloging-in-Publication Data is available
on the Library of Congress website.

ISBN: 978-1-4965-9797-7 (library binding)
ISBN: 978-1-4965-9801-1 (ebook PDF)

Summary: Dan wants the X-9000 high-top sneakers more than
anything. So when a hooded figure leaves a brand-new pair on
the city bus, Dan grabs them and doesn't look back. But the
shoes seem to have a mind of their own . . .

Editor: Abby Huff
Designer: Brann Garvey
Production Specialist: Katy LaVigne

Printed and bound in the USA.
PA117

THE HAUNTED HIGH-TOPS

BY
ROSIE KNIGHT

ILLUSTRATED BY
FRAN BUENO

WORD OF WARNING:

YOU SHOULDN'T TAKE WHAT ISN'T YOURS.

6

After school...

"Where did you get them? The lunchroom trash?" Ugh.

Whhhooooaaaaa.

The X-9000s.

They're so cool... If I had a pair, Rob and Todd would have to shut their big mouths.

But they're so expencive. Mom will never be able to afford them. And I'll never get to wear them.

SCREECH!!

11

13

After school...

The X-9000s *did* change everything. Rob and Todd admitted I'm cool. I won that race. People *noticed* me.

After what Jen said, I felt bad about taking them. But now it feels like fate!

BIRK BIRK BIRK

Calm down, doggo. It's okay.

What? My leg—what's happening?

BIRK BIRK BIRK BIRK

BIRK BIRK BIRK BIRK

The next day...

There's definitely something off about you. But I can't just toss a pair of X-9000s!

But I also can't wear you again till I know what's going on.

Dan!

Hey, I'm sorry about yesterday. It sounds weird, but those shoes were creeping me out.

Oh! You got rid of them?

Yeah... I got rid of them.

Cool!

And the square root of 666 equals...

TAP TAP

Sit down!

They're gone! They're really gone!

I'm free!

The next day, and everything is back to normal...

And then he just disappeared!

LOL, of course he did. See, I knew you just had to give them back!

I'm so glad to see you two hanging out again! Perfect timing, since...

1. Even before the X-9000s reappear on Dan's feet, there are signs the shoes are trouble. Flip through the story and find three spots in the text and art that hint at their true nature.

2. Why is the art wavy in these panels from page 19? What is going on in the story? Brainstorm other ways the art could be drawn to set this moment apart.

3. What's making the *KNOCK* sounds here? How do you know that? Turn to pages 19–20 if you need help.

4. Why do you think Dan lies to Jen about getting rid of the shoes? In your own words, describe why he hangs on to them for so long.

5. At the end of the story, the shoes come back! Will Dan ever be able to get rid of them? Write what happens next.

THE AUTHOR

Rosie Knight has been writing all her life. Growing up in London, she was an avid reader and later became a professional poet until she moved to Los Angeles to write comics. She's the author of *Fierce Heroines* and also an award-winning journalist who writes about films, books, comics, and TV at sites like *The Hollywood Reporter, Nerdist, IGN*, and *Esquire*. Rosie has always loved spooky stories and wrote her first horror novella at age 13! She currently lives the dream life, writing for a living and watching old scary movies with her husband in Long Beach, California.

THE ILLUSTRATOR

Fran Bueno is a comic artist with more than twenty-five years of experience. He graduated in Fine Arts from the Complutense University of Madrid and has worked on a wide variety of projects since then, illustrating for advertisements, children's books, and young adult comics. In addition, he is an instructor at the O Garaxe Hermético Professional School of Comics where he teaches traditional inking and graphic skills. He lives in Santiago de Compostela, Spain.

GLOSSARY

afford (uh-FOHRD)—to have enough money to buy something

creepy (KREE-pee)—weird or a little scary in a way that makes you feel nervous

curse (KUHRS)—an evil spell put onto someone or something that is meant to harm others

defeat (di-FEET)—to win over someone or something

deserve (di-ZUHRV)—to earn something based on your actions

doomed (DOOMD)—likely to have a terrible or unhappy ending

expensive (ik-SPEN-siv)—costing a lot of money

fate (FAYT)—a power believed to control what happens to people

haunted (HAWN-ted)—having a spirit stay with a thing or in a place, often in a way that causes strange things to happen

style (STILE)—the way in which a person dresses

trendy (TREN-dee)—what is popular at that moment

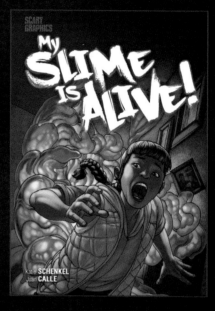
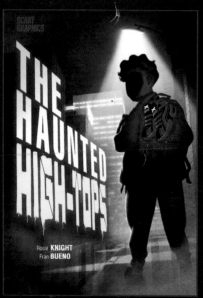